The Thanksgiving Bowl

The Thanksgiving Bowl

By Virginia Kroll

Illustrated by Philomena O'Neill

PELICAN PUBLISHING COMPANY
Gretna 2009

For my cherished great-niece, Tori Frederick,
and my young friend, Tyler Herman

Copyright © 2007
By Virginia Kroll

Illustrations copyright © 2007
By Philomena O'Neill
All rights reserved

First printing, August 2007
Second printing, April 2009

The word "Pelican" and the depiction of a pelican
are trademarks of Pelican Publishing Company, Inc.,
and are registered in the U.S. Patent and Trademark Office.

Library of Congress Cataloging-in-Publication Data

Kroll, Virginia L.
  The Thanksgiving bowl / Virginia Kroll; illustrated by Philomena O'Neill.
     p. cm.
  Summary: Each member of a family writes an anonymous "I Am Thankful For" note and places it in the Thanksgiving bowl, but after the family guesses who wrote each note, the bowl is accidentally left outside, where it rolls off on a year-long series of adventures.
  ISBN 978-1-58980-365-7 (hardcover : alk. paper)
  [1. Thanksgiving Day—Fiction. 2. Bowls (Tableware)—Fiction.] I. O'Neill, Philomena, ill. II. Title.
  PZ7.K9227Th 2007
  [E]—dc22

                                        2007007070

Printed in Singapore
Published by Pelican Publishing Company, Inc.
1000 Burmaster Street, Gretna, Louisiana 70053

THE THANKSGIVING BOWL

Thanksgiving Day dawned on a sunny town. At Grandma Grace's big white house, tummy-tempting smells greeted her family as they came from their faraway homes.

The yellow plastic "Thanksgiving" bowl sat on the front-hall table beside a pad and pencil so that they all could jot down their "I Am Thankful For" things.

Hours after the supper of roast turkey, chestnut stuffing, mashed potatoes, brown gravy, green beans, sweet corn, boiled yams, and cranberry sauce, Grandma Grace announced, "It's time."

Since this Thanksgiving was unusually warm, Grandma Grace and the other grownups served pumpkin pie smothered with whipped cream outside on the picnic table. And in their usual tradition, Grandma read each "I Am Thankful For" aloud while everyone else guessed who had written it.

She unfolded the first one and read, "I am thankful for my cuddly calico, Annie-Cat, who came to stay last spring."

"Sara!" several folks guessed. Sara smiled, thinking of Annie's soft fur and soothing purr.

Another one read, "I am thankful for leftovers so that the feast doesn't have to end today."

"Jeremy!" the cousins yelled. The tall teenager bowed.

After each "I Am Thankful For," baby Joshy clapped his chubby hands and said, "Me, too," which made everyone laugh.

The very last slip of paper said, "I am thankful that everyone I love is thankful."

"Grandma Grace!" shouted a chorus of voices.

As the sun went down, the wind kicked up. Grownups grabbed plates, forks, and cups, and everyone rushed inside. The Thanksgiving bowl tumbled to the ground unnoticed.

Across the road to the Rooneys' farm it rolled, bumping through rows of cornstalk stubble and wilted pumpkin vines. Finally, it lodged upside down between two low bushes at the far end of the field.

On a chilly December night, when the field was awash with the light of the Full Cold Moon, a meadow mouse scampered about, nibbling left-behind seeds. Suddenly she saw a silent-winged barn owl coming toward her. The mouse *eeeked* and scurried away as the barn owl bore down.

Oh! But what was that brightly colored object? The mouse squeezed under the yellow plastic bowl just as the barn owl's talon scraped it. Whew! The bowl had a comforting smell and a cozy feel about it, so the mouse hunkered down, wrapped her tail around herself, and slept until she could safely get away. When she pushed her way out, the yellow plastic bowl turned right side up and went rolling away in the wind again.

On a blustery January "snow day" from school, Brad and Jeff found the bowl by their garage when they went out to make a snowman. "What a perfect hat!" Jeff said, so *plunk* it went on the snowman's head.

In February, during an unexpected thaw, the yellow plastic bowl floated in the used-to-be-a-snowman puddle till a breeze sent it rolling to a hill above a rushing stream. Two curious otters saw it and got in. *Whee!* They slid swiftly down the hill in their "flying saucer," bumping against a rock and tumbling out at the shore. The water carried the Thanksgiving bowl away.

It didn't take long for a pair of Canada geese to find the bowl. In March, the female piled grasses into it, then cushioned it with moss and soft down feathers. She kept her five eggs warm in the bowl while her mate stood guard.

When their fuzzy goslings were two days old, they led them to the water—and not a second too soon, for a hungry fox came gosling-hunting. He flipped the empty nest upside down, then hurried off in an angry huff.

Shaylyn found the Thanksgiving bowl as she hunted for fossils in April. She carried them home in it. Her friend, Alexandra, said, "That bowl would be the perfect pot for my plant project," so Shaylyn gave it to her.

Alexandra filled it with soil, pushed in her striped seeds, and kept them watered in a sunny window.

"Happy Mother's Day, Mom," Alexandra said in May. She helped Mom plant four sturdy sunflower seedlings under their back-hall window.

The Thanksgiving bowl blew again, over the lawn and down the road to Pine Tree Pond. In June, Tori squealed, "Tadpoles!" She spotted the bowl, scooped seven tadpoles into it, and took them to school. There she and the other third graders watched them every day till they turned into full-fledged frogs. Tori brought the frogs back to the pond in the yellow plastic bowl and let them go.

The bowl found its way across the highway to an apartment building. Alyssa used it as a boat to float her doll, Denise, in her wading pool on a sweltering July afternoon.

That evening, a gusty thunderstorm took the bowl across a field next door, where it tumbled between rows of ripe red tomatoes and sweet green peppers.

In August, the bowl wound up in Christopher's sand-
box. He and his best friend, Noah, used it as a mold to
build a grand castle for their knights and dragons.

In September, Christopher's mom raked her yard and added the bowl to her bin for recycling plastic. The bowl fell off the recycling truck when Mr. Bacon, the trash collector, hit a bump. It rolled all the way to Tyler's backyard. "Are you big enough to fill the bird feeder?" his grandpa asked him. Tyler stood on tippytoes but wasn't quite tall enough. Then he turned over the Thanksgiving bowl, used it as a stepstool, and reached just right.

Looking for food in late October, a mother raccoon and her three playful kits discovered the yellow plastic bowl and decided to investigate. They prodded it and pushed it around, past the Rooneys' farm and across the road. When they got hungry, they left it in a pile of orange leaves in front of a big white house.

On Thanksgiving Day, Grandma Grace's family pulled into the driveway once again. Toddler Joshy spotted something in the yard and ran to get it. He came back a second later wearing a yellow plastic hat. He marched proudly into the house, declaring, "I a builder. My helmet."

"Mercy!" Grandma Grace exclaimed. "I've been looking all over for that. Wherever did you find my Thanksgiving bowl?"

"Right where we left it last year," Sara answered.

"Hmmm." Grandma Grace looked puzzled. Then she smiled and opened her arms for warm, tight, sweet-smelling Thanksgiving hugs.